LET'S BE BUDDIES
A JEFFERSON BALL ADVENTURE

by David Perlmutter

LET'S BE BUDDIES: A JEFFERSON BALL ADVENTURE

David Perlmutter

I.

Hamilton Pomeranian- formerly Major Hamilton Pomeranian of the Star Soldiers- looked slowly and bitterly out the airlock window of the starship that was returning her to Earth, after a period of (at least what she felt was) meritorious service. She was not exactly pleased to be leaving it sooner than she desired, since it was not under the circumstances or on the terms that she desired. That was never the case with the Star Soldiers, unless you were fortunate enough to gain an upper tier command position, and that was a very rare circumstance when you started from the bottom, as Hamilton had.

Yet, considering all the difficulties she had encountered over the course of her career, particularly with the males who gave her grief and insulted her intelligence far too often, and her growing lack of patience with this, it was probably for the best that she exited this self-enclosed military caste now, before self-loathing increasingly got the best of her.

She had been forcibly retired due to injuries, according to the protocol she had understood and acted upon during her ten years' tenure in the force. She knew that this would be inevitable from the time she had first registered pain on duty, for this was simply the way in which things "worked". The Star Soldiers- arguably the "finest" of the chiefly canine citizens of Earth of the fourth millennium- had no place for anyone showing anything remotely like physical or mental weakness, and were quick to show offenders the door when that happened. Whether or not they liked it- and often, like Hamilton, they didn't.

So Hamilton knew automatically, in her time of peril, that she was doomed. The extent of her injuries fully and completely established the fact that she would now be useless to the Soldiers. Even though she still had her mind and wits, those things were nothing to them without a completely healthy body with which to undertake assignments and commands. Which, in their mind, was the only thing that those under their tight-pawed control were really good for, anyway.

That, however, did not make Hamilton any less bitter about the capricious nature by which she had been discharged. All *that* did was give her another very good reason to hate them all.

Happy to rid herself of the itchy red and black wool clothing that comprised a Soldiers' uniform, Hamilton was now back in the civilian clothes she had entered the service in- as a naïve and somewhat star struck teenager straight from high school- and which she favored as often as she could on her rarely granted leaves. These consisted of a white T shirt that struck a contrasting chord with her bright yellow fur, a black leather motorcycle cap put at a jaunty angle on her head, a pair of sweat pants with a camouflage pattern, and a pair of open-toed sandals- the better to show off her small, still very canine feet. It was much better, she had found, to be dressed as a civilian when trying to pick up one night stands on leave, for, like her, civilians found the formal Star Soldiers uniform a turn off. Not surprising, considering what those in uniform had done while wearing them in the outer planets.

While not technically a prisoner, Hamilton felt as if she had been put in the brig most of this voyage. Protocol prevented her, as a now ex-member of the force, from openly communicating with any of the crew in a friendly fashion, and from moving much beyond the quarters she had been assigned on this ship. Now that she was a "foreigner", as they called non-members of the force, she was, as a result, in a possible position to influence the members with the kind of forthright, independently-minded thought that they believed was anathema to the force's good health, and which they clamped down on whenever any possibility of its actual or perceived presence occurred to them.

Hamilton's forced imprisonment thus created an atmosphere for much thought and contemplation, and she took full advantage of that to contemplate her past position within the ranks, as well as what, if any, position she might possibly be able to hold in the new Earth she was returning to after such a long time away.

Most of that time, her thoughts had been directed towards the rapid chain of events that ultimately led to the downfall of her military career. She had been on duty, commanding, as was due her hardearned rank, a hardscrabble unit in a distant far-away quadrant of the universe, with "uncivilized" residents and unchecked "barbarism", by the Soldiers' standards, reining supreme.

She had earned both friends and enemies within her ranks, as she had everywhere she had served as an officer, for both her all-business attitude on the job and her more relaxed one (conditioned by the bacchanalian benefits accorded a Soldier off-duty) when she was not required to "turn on" the more serious parts of her life and job. But all the serious plotting, planning, and worrying she did about keeping her "guys" and "gals" safe doing their job at all times, again as she always had done, proved to be for naught in this particular case. From out of nowhere, the unit was ambushed by the alien beings who called the quadrant home, and which the Soldiers were, in vain, trying to keep under control. In the ensuing scuffle, several members of the unit received wounds. Not fatal ones, it should be said, but bad enough ones to permanently impair their physical and/or mental abilities.

Hamilton, being shorter than most of her larger colleagues, ended up coming in for a wider share of the injuries than they did, as she was in closer range of the enemy's weapons when they began to use them. She lost her vision entirely in her right eye, and had bones completely destroyed in her left leg, so that, for ever after, she would walk with a permanent, noticeable limp.

Of course, they *had* to have a Court Martial after that. That was what they did every time there was a remote screw-up in the ranks, just to make sure that everyone knew stupidity and incompetence would not be tolerated, even though they were quite obviously sure that it did not already. Also of course,

Hamilton, as the commanding officer, was the one who ended up shouldering the blame for the incident and its heavily consequential aftermath. She defended herself as best as she could when called up to testify, but, as she very well knew, she was fighting a losing battle. Not surprisingly, she was convicted, and her punishment, as was typical for a commanding officer in a similar position to hers, was immediate discharge. Though she was going out with the substantial benefits accorded to a being of her rank and experience, including a large yearly pension that would supplement her income for the remainder of her life, there would always be- at least among the internalized crowd of the Star Soldiers- the stain of what she had done, or had *not* done, within the construction of her public image, such as it would be. Her only choice was to live with it, but *liking* it was another matter.

*

Eventually, her period of contemplation came to an abrupt end.

The ship arrived on Earth, and rapidly entered the planet's orbit, with the gravitational fluctuation to prove it. Hamilton gripped the edges of the chair on which she sat tightly to prevent being thrown hither and yon in the process of descent and landing, which was accomplished at a very fast clip. Eventually, the vessel stabilized and was still. Those aboard could now disembark if they wished.

Hamilton definitely *wanted* to disembark.

She was about to get up and leave, when she heard a knock at the door of her chamber.

"Are you in there, Major Pomeranian?" said a voice, although this was asked redundantly in the extreme.

She went to the door and opened it. There, by the looks of his face, was a very young and inexperienced soldier, obviously dispatched by his superiors to inform her of the "good" news regarding the ship's landing. He was much taller than her, the kind she liked on the rare occasions when she was allowed to fully act on her sexual urges. And the way he looked in uniform....but she had to dispatch those kinds of thoughts from her mind, now that she was simply a civilian. That kind of romantic relationship was frowned upon amongst the Soldiers. For good reasons, as she well knew.

"Yes?" she asked.

"We've arrived," he said. "You can leave now, if you wish."

Hamilton went and grabbed the sack containing the few valuable things she had, and hoisted it over her shoulders, like an old fashioned tramp with a bindle, in the old human Earth days, as she left the room.

"Oh, I *wish*," she said, bitterly. "I *wish* I'd never gotten involved with you *guys* in the first place, too. If you get my *meaning, kid*."

"Do you want me to...?"

"No!"

She sounded curt, more than she planned to be, but it was enough for him to stand at attention respectfully and not bother her, as she wanted.

"I'm not *disabled*," she continued. "I can manage well enough on my own. But thank you very *kindly* for being *concerned* about me. Your kind of kindness was entirely *absent* when I got Court-Martialed!"

Word of the wounds she had suffered had obviously traveled fast among the crew of the ship, despite her not interacting with them on the voyage, and so they were quick to their feet once they saw her entering the chambers, to attempt to "assist" her. She waved them all off, brusquely.

"Don't *bother*," she said, repeatedly. "I'm not your *problem* anymore. Besides, I can find my own way off this tub fairly easily. I've spent enough time on them to know how they work. In fact, I probably know more about them than any of you *ever* will. But do any of *you* really care about what *I* think, now that

I'm not your damned *problem* anymore? I should say NOT! Good riddance to bad rubbish!"

She finally reached the airlock of the ship, walked through it, and entered the atmosphere of a planet that, although she was a native of, seemed as alien to her as any other she'd visited, since she had been away from it for so long.

A period of adjustment and reintegration was thus, she thought to herself, both mandatory and necessary.

*

And so it was that Hamilton Pomeranian, ex-Star Soldier and now civilian, found herself wandering the streets of Hugopolis, the major city of this new Earth. Like so many others newly arrived to the place, she now sought lodgings and work, and was not certain of gaining either, at least not immediately. Even the advanced- and somewhat revered- status of being one of the supposedly all-powerful and invincible Star Soldiers was no guarantee of that. In some cases, particularly among the more liberal minded who believed the force to be a waste of time and money, this was exactly the thing that would permanently end any chances of gaining employment or residence she might want, need or desire. And then there were her war "wounds", which would serve as a further obstacle in that regard....

These uncomfortable realities, which now came to replace the concern for her troops' safety that had previously occupied much of her waking and subconscious thoughts, loosened feelings of anger in her that, until now, had been hidden or suppressed. Quickly and violently, she unloosened a fusillade of rage that exploded out of her mouth like a torrent.

"*Damn* it!" she swore. "I gave those creeps the best years of my life! I did *everything* they told me to, *exactly* like they told me to do it, *all* the time. Hell! I was such a goddamned "exemplary" figure that they *had* to commend me *every* time I got a promotion, like I was some sort of *saint*. But the moment- the exact *moment*- I pulled a boner- which was nothing I had any *control* over, *thank you*- and get myself *injured*, well, *then* they just pretend I never existed, and sweep me under the rug! Those stupid boneheaded BOYS! If they weren't being "kind" enough to pension me off the way they did, why, I'd...."

Her monologue was interrupted when another "boy" crossed her path. This was not a soldier, however, but a common criminal. Of the desperate nature that the majority of criminals were even in that futuristic time, though he took great pains to disguise it with the most aggressive of manners.

He indicated his social status most clearly when he stepped right in Hamilton's path, whipped out a long knife, and directed it in the vicinity of her stomach. He was a figure much bigger than her, but she was used to that by now. So used to it, in fact, that she barely batted an eyelid when he jumped in front of her. She knew perfectly well how to deal with ruffians, from plenty of past experience, and she hoped that she could draw on the same well of experience to deal with him the same way.

"Well?" he prompted, in a typical, guttural criminal fashion.

It was an old routine for him, and he thought he'd get the proper answer for it. She, however, was unfamiliar with the demand, at least the way they did on Earth, due to her extended absence. She looked at him with bemusement, like someone willing to let somebody else act out a well-worn comedy routine that had lost much of its charm through repeated, dry and mechanical repetition.

Until she shocked him by delivering the punchline much better than he ever could.

"Well, *what?*" she answered, putting her burden down on the ground. "Explain yourself, please."

"I think you know."

"I think I *don't.*"

He was nonplussed. Not used to having extended conversations with his victims, by any means, he tried another tactic.

"You're not from here?" he asked.

"Well, I was born here, and grew up here, if that's what you mean." she said, without breaking a sweat. "I've been off-planet for a while. Work and all that. But I can tell, exactly, what it is you want. They make your kind all over the galaxy."

"So you're a Star Soldier, huh?"

"Yeah. Just got out. How'd you guess?"

"They come down this way, often. The space station's not too far from here. They end up coming down this way when they're in town."

Remaking his original point, he put his knife perpendicular to her navel once again.

"*And* they're the only kind of people in this here neighborhood that would have a remote chance of having anything *valuable*. On their bodies, in their wallets, or anywhere else they might want to try to *hide* whatever it is they got on them. Is that clear enough for you to understand?"

"Certainly. But, as you said, I'm a Star Soldier. So I know *exactly* how to deal with you."

"How?"

"Like *this*."

She reached into her pocket for her gun, the formidably locked and loaded weapon assigned to each Star Soldier on and off duty in cases like this. When other Soldiers- or, more likely, civilians, when they got drunk and thought they could get "lucky" owing to the "easy" reputation many Soldiers had- made life more difficult than it needed to be for them. The threat of being shot, with the expert marksmanship that each Soldier was required to have, was enough to scare most ruffians off without the Soldier even being required to fire the weapon at all. This was the effect Hamilton was hoping for: to drive the threat away. At least away from her.

But it was not to be.

It was only after that rash action that she remembered that, as one of the conditions of her discharge, she was forced to return her weapon to the quartermaster before she boarded the ship for her return voyage to Earth.

Therefore, *she no longer had anything with which to defend herself*!

Beneath her yellow fur, she turned pale. A fact not unnoticed by her potential assailant.

"*Forgot* something?" the robber asked. To which Hamilton could only nod in fear.

"Good," he grinned. "That'll make this a lot easier."

She tried to evade him by moving fast, backwards, but he came closer to her with every step. Her doom seemed ever-evident with each advance.

*

The would-be assault was, however, interrupted.

It came in the form of a high-pitched, shrill whistle. Both parties assumed that it had nothing to do with them, and so continued as before, even when a second whistle cut through the air. The relevance of the audio display to the robbery in progress was only made clear when a voice, calling from the same direction as the whistle, called out towards the robber.

"Hey! Fathead!" it said. "Turn around and come down this way a bit!"

The robber did so. And, as he did, he realized that the events of the day were *not* going to go as he planned, after all.

The being who was the source of the voice made itself known.

Hamilton could only see the encounter from a distance, but, even with her limited vision, she could tell right away that the being was as feminine as she was. She was, however, much larger in size than Hamilton (and, more importantly, the robber) and had greater endowments of femininity, which she displayed in what appeared to be a bikini and boots, both colored black. She quickly disarmed the robber, breaking the knife in half, depositing the handle in a nearby trash can, and then, with a bold air of confident, seductive menace, picked her fangs with the blade before disposing of it in the same fashion.

Before the robber had even a remote chance of being able to evade her, she put both of her paws around his neck, seemingly with the intent of choking him to death. She seemed to have all the enormous, formidable kind of strength in her body that would allow her to accomplish that incredible feat.

"I don't appreciate it when I have *friends* nearly robbed on the street," she told him. "It's bad enough that I have to rescue complete strangers from the likes of *you*. But when it comes to people I know well, it's a *bigger* problem."

She released him from her grip, and kicked him pointing the other way on the pavement, implying that he was to make himself scarce as soon as he possibly could.

"Don't let me catch you here again," the bikini-clad marvel warned him. "Especially not with *her*. She is, as I just said, a *friend* of mine. And it won't pay for you to mess around with any of my friends, or else you'll be lying down on this pavement, *bleeding* to death. *Understand*?"

He did. He fled immediately, without another word. The message had come across, loud and clear.

Then, the oversized avenger- or criminal, or whatever she truly was- proceeded towards Hamilton.

That set off another wave of panic in the smaller dog. She'd just gotten out of being robbed by this creature. Was it now, actually, to happen, at the threat of her formidable paws?

For Hamilton clearly had no means of defending herself against this larger figure any more than she had against her previous assailant. Certainly not with the stranger outclassing her in size, weight and strength, and Hamilton having no access to the one thing that could equalize them.

Yet all was resolved, after a fashion, when the larger figure approached her with a much more familiar, and definitely friendlier, gait in her step.

Now Hamilton could see clearly that her fur was brown, including a portion that had grown around and covered her ears like a human head of hair, and her bikini had the monogram "JB" on both parts in white on it. In all, she was a tall, beautiful, strong, athletic, and quick figure—something that Hamilton only wished she could be. Especially now that her own body had been so grievously compromised.

Hamilton, however, was still on guard, like the soldier she had until recently been, and as she would be until she knew she was free and clear of any danger. She couldn't exactly be sure of what was being demanded of her until such a demand was said, after all.

II.

"Hamilton!" the large, over-eager figure exclaimed, with a cheerful and friendly tone now emerging in her commanding voice. "How *are* you?"

Well, that settled it. At least, up to a point. The creature obviously knew Hamilton, although Hamilton herself had never seen her before. It could simply be somebody who knew of her only vaguely, from the minor heroics of her prior career, and wanted to settle some prior score, with themselves, or possibly a friend or relation, that had receded from the smaller dog's memory over time. Hamilton remained tense until such time as she felt she could be at ease.

"Do I *know* you?" she demanded of the larger figure, suspiciously.

That made the other pause and open her mouth, incredulously, before she spoke again.

"Well!" she said, insulted. "You *should*. Going through the basic *hell* of basic training for the Star Soldiers should make you have at least a cursory memory of the people you went *through* it with."

"I remember who I went through basic training with very well, *thank you*," retorted Hamilton, losing her patience. "And I don't recall anyone of your.....stature....being among those folks."

"Can I help it if I've changed? That was a few years ago. A lot can happen in a period of years."

"You're darn right about that," said Hamilton, in rueful reflection. "But it still doesn't explain to me who you are, and what you want with me. Knowing that would take an awful lot off my mind."

"Oh, come on!" The being put her forepaws together. "We were, like, *this* close. How could you possibly forget somebody who you were that close with? I didn't have any other friends there. I depended on you to help me, seeing you were the only other girl in our group. And you did. You were the closest friend I ever had then, and probably ever will have. I didn't forget you. Not for a second. Not ever since then. Why did *you* forget about *me*?"

"Like you said, a lot can happen in a few years. You can't keep track of everything that happens to you easily- or every*one,* for that matter. But I do owe you my gratitude, and I shouldn't be detaining myself from expressing that to you. So thank you, for preventing me from going through what could have been a very difficult situation..."

"Ah, gratitude." The larger dog bowed chivalrously. "The greatest pleasure I can get from providing my assistance to a fellow being. Thank you, in return. I was just doing my job, and it needed to be done, in your case. You're right. It could have been difficult, but I took care of that, didn't I?"

"Well, of course I'm grateful. But it'd help me a great deal if I knew exactly who I was dealing with, and how it is we happen to know each other from the past. Or, should I say, *you* do, and I've forgotten about
it."

"Gladly."

The figure turned around, and spoke to Hamilton in wistful, bitter reflection.

"When you entered basic training," she said, "you came right out of high school, didn't you? Well, there was another one like you there, who was just as young, and came in to the ranks just fresh from getting her high school diploma, just like you had. She didn't have any obvious options for a career other than the military, the same way you had the same sort of limited career options, and those two things helped the two of you bond. Like right quick. You stay bonded until you were forcibly separated. But I'll get to all of that in a moment.

"The girl in question wasn't what you would call physically attractive, or tall. But you didn't care about that. You were in the same boat all the way in nearly everything, only you looked a little bit better. All you saw was somebody being snubbed and ignored just for not meeting some stupid standard or other, and you couldn't stand that. You befriended her, and she was eternally grateful for that. You roomed together and all that stuff, and you didn't mind being the butt of jokes for hanging around with her all the time. Besides, when you actually started doing the physical and mental training, you found out that she actually was smart, strong and athletic. As much as you in the physical departments, but not as much in the mental stuff, which was where you had to help her with the problems she had. To put it another way, you were her best friend.

"The one big problem she had was that she was as disrespectful and as disobedient as hell. She just wasn't interested in doing things if there was nothing for her as an immediate reward waiting beyond that. The Soldiers, as you know, aren't about that sort of thing, and so they pushed back each and every time she tried to express herself and her individuality, particularly out in public. So she rebelled. Softly and quietly at first, but, eventually, after one too many sessions in KP as punishment, she lost it. One day, she just stopped doing anything she was told that even remotely resembled an order- which, of course, was everything they said. One of the corporals got so fed up with her behavior that he slapped her in the face to try to make her "behave" like they wanted her to. It backfired, to put it rather simply. She beat the stuffing out of him, completely cleaned his clock, and left him for dead out in the street, almost like he *was* dead. Only thing was, he wasn't, and he got back at her good the only way he felt was

fair.

"You, meanwhile were outraged that she had done this, for it was the sort of thing that disrupted the "flow" of "action" you and all the rest of them were so damned concerned with then. You spoke to her harshly about the incident, and what consequences might result for her. You tried to make her understand the grave error that she had committed.

But she had a vainglorious attitude towards herself, to say nothing of a very stubborn nature and a fat head to go along with it. She wouldn't even begin to believe that what she did could be somehow interpreted as an error. She was defending herself after her honor as a female being had been insulted by a male who thought he could take advantage of her.

That was all.

"Not even when she received the inevitable summons to appear at the Court Martials they call at the drop of a hat whenever somebody supposedly acts more uppity than they like did she recant her story or modify her attitude. She disgraced herself so much in the eyes of the high command there, what with her irreverent attitude towards the whole proceedings, that they knew right then and there that she did not belong in the Star Soldiers. Then, there, or *ever*. Not only was she dismissed on the spot, without any preliminaries or formalities, but she also had the unprecedented "honor" of being imprisoned for nearly a year afterwards before it was finally felt she could be of some loosely defined "benefit" to society at large.

"Which, debatably, she eventually became. Here and now.

"You lost track of her after that. But you never entirely forgot her, as you went along in your career. The career she never got to have.

"Her name- or, at least, someone having the same name as her- kept coming up every once in a while as the star figure in some heroic fight or other in a far-away corner of the wide and mysterious galaxy, as a secretive, muscle-bound righter of wrongs wherever and whenever she saw them happening, or as some intergalactic "fixer" for big problems. You might have seen her name in the electronic papers, with or without an accompanying picture. As you read about her exploits, and what she seemed capable of doing with the amazing powers she seemed to have acquired out of nowhere, you probably might have re-evaluated your choice to join the Star Soldiers and live by their imperfect rules and regs. But, if you ever brought yourself to do that, it didn't last long. You just weren't that type, and still aren't. That thing was your life, and maybe still is. You have that kind of craving for order, and organization, and power gained at a gradual rather than immediate level, that she never had, and never will.

"If you haven't guessed what her name is by now, I guess I'm going to have to give it to you to straighten things out. Her name is-"

"Jefferson Ball!" interrupted Hamilton.

For, indeed, the extended monologue had opened her eyes to who, exactly, was now addressing her.

As the figure recounted events in her own life- and Hamilton's- with an astonishing amount of pure clarity and detail, there could not be any more dispute about exactly who this was. It was a dear and precious acquaintance from a previous path in her life, and, despite a vast and still unexplained change in experience, it could not possibly be any other being. Hamilton responded to this epiphany by rushing as quickly as she could to the side of her friend, and embracing her tightly around the few parts of her body that she could touch, coupling this with a genial, girlish laugh that Jefferson soon copied.

After Hamilton broke free from her, Jefferson continued the affectionate physicality by putting her paw on Hamilton's head.

"Gosh!" Hamilton observed, when that little affectionate display ended. "How could it be I didn't recognize you right away?"

"Well, I told you," Jefferson reminded her. "I changed."

"Obviously," answered Hamilton, craning her neck for a better look at her friend. "But *how*? You used to be only slightly taller than I was, and now..."

"You not only forgot about me," said Jefferson, "but about my family. Remember what I said about them?"

"Right," Hamilton recollected. "The *changes*."

Jefferson Ball came from a long line of what were once scientifically called "mutants", and vulgarly called "freaks", first among the long vanished human population, and then amongst the semi-human canine beings who replaced them in the march of evolution, of which Jefferson and Hamilton were very obvious current examples. The march of change started with Jefferson's earliest known ancestors, who were involved in the more far-out ends of the last major phase of scientific experimentation before the human race finally obliterated itself, in a seemingly endless supply of nuclear weapon-laced wars and similarly brutal internal rebellions and revolutions. These included major- and often misguided- efforts to give the "lower" animals all the "benefits" which human beings had accorded themselves, over numerous centuries, in their rapid rise to dominance of the world- and their equally rapid decline. Among these were a "straightener" of the spine to make those of lower creatures vertical rather than horizontal in the movement of their bodies; a similar conversion of legs into upper and lower limbs; and a laborious, but eventually successful, attempt to replace the barks, whines and growls of the original canine races with (imperfect) English speech. With the latter, much of the diction and delivery of the source language remained in place, as is common in the speaking of any language one is not fluent in.

While many of these efforts were conducted by groups of scientists rather than singular ones in laboratories (whose locations were hidden to avoid potentially bloody confrontations with those who continued to vociferously defend the "rights" of the subjects), one scientist went further than all the rest on his own. Through a Mendelian manipulation of the genes of dogs he had meticulously "mapped", carefully bred, and, through the aforementioned innovations, "woke" into humanity, he was able to successfully create a long line of very human-like dogs. Unfortunately, these beings still had much of their ancient wolf-pack mentality in their heads, and they, consequently, interpreted everyone around them as prey, and killed those around them as such- including him.

It took some time for the human aspects of the personalities ingrained in their genetics to stand up to and control the canine ones, and even this could often be only a temporary and extremely tense *détente*. But, eventually, this came to pass.

By then, this canine race had ravaged the planet and destroyed mankind. Yet it did not result in the vast wasteland that the final humans feared would occur once they were gone. Successive generations, as they fully came into the mental consciousness the humans gifted them with, began to discover the benefits and works of the humans, and to assert a full position as their successors. A major part of this was the arrival of a number of alien races, who had belatedly discovered the efforts of the humans of

Earth to contact them in distant periods of the past. The new canine race benefitted deeply from alien knowledge of Earth from popular culture past to build the new faux-human society they most certainly wanted to have, as well as from a healthy exchange of beneficial powers and abilities through interbreeding. The results were now noticeable in healthy, functioning societies on Earth and all of the other known planets and moons, and were particularly on display in the Star Soldiers, one of whose functions was to police and control said societies when local authorities felt they could no longer maintain such control on their own.

The Ball family, while not entirely cut off from the society that had gradually but noticeably given them what in any time would have been considerable physical and mental resources, were descended from the original "imperfect" canine beings created by the scientist who had started this whole mess, and continued to live in the area nearby where those experiments had taken place. However, unlike most of the canine and other anthropomorphic races that now surrounded them, they were not "fixed" in a particular physical or mental appearance for their entire lives. This was due to extreme fluctuations in their genetic makeup, which would become most graphically apparent once the members hit puberty. Members would start their lives looking attractive, and then, just around the time of physical maturity, turn astonishingly ugly for no obvious or explainable reason. Or they would begin their lives being hale and hearty, and then end up and sick and bed-ridden for the remainder. A wide range of fluctuations affected the various members at various times for various reasons, since no two of their genetic patterns, as with the ancient humans, was an exact match. The circumstances of their parentage and the environments in which they brought up in provided additional possibilities for variance.

Jefferson, however, was an oddity among even that bizarre group. She was born ugly and short, and had remained so throughout her childhood and adolescence, as well as in the short but highly memorable stint in the Star Soldiers already described. But, during her imprisonment, and afterwards…. "I knew it was coming," Jefferson explained to Hamilton, as they walked down the street together. "Even when we were first together in basic training, I *knew*. I knew I couldn't be a little butt-ugly slob forever. I was somehow destined for better things. That was why I acted up so much. Why should I stand around and take orders from people who were so….beneath me? Obviously, they interpreted it a little differently.

"But when I was imprisoned, I felt it happening inside of me. I grew whole feet taller. I was getting stronger than I'd ever been, stronger than anyone else. I showed off for the guards by bending the steel bars of my cell, and they were too scared to go near me after that. Later, when I got out, I felt like I could move faster than anyone alive. I ran for blocks at a time, and never felt the kind of winded I used to be in the slightest. So I knew it had happened."

"It happened, all right," agreed Hamilton. "But why the bikini? It might give some people the wrong impression of who you are and what you're trying to do. Especially boys." "I told you that already, silly," Jefferson answered. "It's part of my job."

"Job?"

"Superhero," declared Jefferson. "About the only one I was suited for, given my abilities and my temperament. All the good ones have a uniform of some kind. This is the one I felt I needed to have. That way, folks will know me when I come on the scene, and I won't have to explain myself, to them or anyone else. Besides, being a superhero is the only job that'll let me display my bod the way I want to, and not get any complaints about what I wear from somebody who's making me do a job for pay. This is what I work in, and, since I'm pretty much on the job at all times, it makes sense to leave it on all the time, too. Not that it's just this one. I got plenty of copies at home in the closet, for when I absolutely *have* to change. But I can't go back now. This is my image, my logo, my icon. Even if you have some objections to it, Hamilton, I'm not going back on it. I'm stuck on it now.

"Besides, it's a big improvement over the lousy clothes we had to wear as grunts. You know how much I disliked those shapeless grey sweaters and sweat pants they made us wear all the time in basic training. Now, I live and work free, without worrying about answering to anybody else for anything stupid or misguided I do. Just myself, and I forgive myself for what I do all the time. And you can live like that yourself, if you like, now that you've been discharged."

"But why are you calling being a superhero a 'job'?" Hamilton asked. "A definite and important role in society, certainly. No question about that at all. But an actual, full-time paying *job?*" They stopped walking. Jefferson looked at her friend, incredulously.

"Why shouldn't I call it a job?" Jefferson countered. "I do it for a living, don't I? And a great deal of my work is done on freelance contracts, on Earth and abroad. At the end of a lot of those things, I get paid. That helps me out, since I got bills to pay like everyone else. So why in the world shouldn't I think of the job I do for a living *as* a job?"

"You certainly can think of what you do as a job. Your description of your work complies with how the majority of other people see what they do for a living. That's completely undeniable. However, *my* understanding of the definition of your job, at least back in the days when the humans were still around, was that superheroes did their stuff *pro bono,* all the time, and then took on a day job and a secret identity to pay the bills. At least, the ones who weren't rich, and didn't do that secret identity stuff." Jefferson shook her head.

"Yeah, that's how the humans did it," she explained. "Most of them, anyhow. But it's not exactly the same as the way it was when they were here, Ham. Not by a long shot. It's like they used to tell us in school all the time: we do most of the same things the humans do, but differently."

"So how, may I ask, do we do it differently than how they did it?"

"Basically, I hire myself as a private contractor, also like the humans before they bought it, but that was more towards the end, in their world of business, mostly. I tell people through the computer and phone connection grid that serves as the universe's belt that I'm experienced in fighting crime and the forces of evil- which I am, of course (no point in lying about that)- and that I can bench press so-and-so amount, have an IQ of so-and-so much, can run about x number of kilometers at a time, and put up plenty of photos and spreads from my past adventures, along with a good headshot, to prove that I'm not a fake. From that, people approach me about doing jobs. We negotiate a payment based on what they're willing to give me and what I'm prepared to accept, and nothing outside that. It's unethical to do it otherwise, and that's the last thing that an ethical superhero wants to be thought of. Being on the right side of the good and evil ethical divide is our *raison d'etre,* after all. All expenses, if necessary, are included in the deal, since I don't usually have much scratch on me at any given time, and you know how it's always about the credits everywhere you go in this crazy universe. Then, I get myself to the place, do the job, come back here, and collect my fee. Simple as that.

"Once in a while, I might run into some problem on the home turf, like I did finding you, and I set it right. That's where the misinterpretation about the *pro bono* stuff comes in. The thing was, most of the old school human heroes held themselves to such high ethical standards that they had no idea about how wealthy they could have been if they'd only *tried* to get paid for what they did. Then, maybe, the people who got rich off their backs, publicizing them and distributing their adventures in those old timey comic books and what not, wouldn't have gotten so rich in the first place. Then, there wouldn't have been all those disputes about income inequality, the faking of news reports, and all those worries about what the changing of the climate would and has done to Earth. Then the humans wouldn't have fallen, and we wouldn't be here at all now. Any of us, dogs and aliens alike.

"But that's all too complicated to understand. I barely understood it based on how they talked to me about in school, and I still don't know now."

"Same here," retorted Hamilton, shaking her head. "But you're better off than I am, Jeff. Having a whole career in your life, as hard as it is, is something I certainly can't look forward to, at this moment in time."

"How so? Don't they give you a pension and stuff like that if you serve so many years?"

"Yeah. That's all right. Enough to cover my living expenses and whatnot for each year I stay alive from now on, provided I don't spend all of it at once. I've never been the retiring type, though. I'm still want to work and be active. For a little while, anyway. Before my mind goes the way of my body. But I doubt anyone on Earth will let me do that."

"How do you figure that? At least *you* actually have a legitimate C.V. to fall back on. Not like me."

"Are you kidding? With a *limp*? *And* a dead eye? Fat chance of me being a cop, or a night watcher, or a transit security officer, with those drawbacks. Those are the only civilian jobs I'm qualified to do, seeing as Earth has outsourced all the other ones I could possibly do off-planet. And I don't need to remind you of what the *boys* in all of those highly regarded but seriously overrated "professions" think of any girl who tries to do "their" job "better" than them."

"You don't. Most of 'em are only good for one thing related to us, and, even then, they can't get *that* right most of the time."

They both snickered softly, and knowingly, for a moment, before Hamilton sat down on a conveniently placed tree stump and resumed her former melancholia, while Jefferson stood over her.

"On top of that," continued Hamilton, "I got nowhere to stay now. You know I'm an only child, same as you, right? Well, I lost my parents while I was in the service, just like you did when we were together, only this happened after you were discharged. So I can't go back to that old house. Too many memories.

Good ones for sure, but the bad ones started to outnumber them the older I got. Besides, they sold it after I left. So it's not like I have anywhere to go right now."

"Well, it's a good thing you ran into me, then. My apartment house has had a vacancy for as long as I've been staying there. I'm sure that I could put in a good word for you. They'd probably like you better than they do me, since that pension means you'd never have trouble paying your rent on time." "Thank you, Jeff," said Hamilton, brightly and sincerely. "I'd appreciate that very much."

"And don't be concerned about not getting a job. I think I can solve that problem also." "Really?"

"Yeah. It's not that difficult, and you're more that qualified to do it, never mind those disabilities of yours. You can be my sidekick."

Unexpectedly, and very quickly, Hamilton became fully enraged.

Despite the vast difference in their sizes, strength and physical capability, the smaller dog leapt off the stump and pushed her larger colleague with a great deal of force into a nearby fence. Jefferson crashed down to the ground quickly, in the process destabilizing and collapsing the fence beneath her. When she was down, and before she could say anything in return, Hamilton stood over her viciously, ready to pounce for the kill at any moment.

"Is *that* all I am to you?" she snarled. "*Seriously?* Somebody you can just *use* for a night, and then throw away? You should know *better* than that, Jefferson. I made that perfectly clear to you more than once when other people tried to do it with me, and I turned them down *flat*. And that was *before* I had my little "accident". *Now,* you probably think I've changed, because I'm supposedly weaker and more vulnerable. And more *desperate,* besides that. Well, I'm NOT! I have a long and decorated military career behind me, and, with that, a reputation that I worked a long time to establish and build. I cannot and I *will* not jeopardize that to become a glorified *servant. Especially* if all you want me for is on those rare occasions when *you* want a jolly good-..."

During Hamilton's speech, Jefferson had gained her feet again, and now she put her paw over

Hamilton's muzzle to prevent her from speaking any further for a moment, before releasing it.

"What," Jefferson demanded, curtly, "are you *talking* about?"

"You called me a sidekick," said Hamilton, as if that explained everything.

"So?" Jefferson said, innocently. "Is that supposed to be a *bad* thing, now?"

"*You* should...."

Then Hamilton realized her mistake. Jefferson had never advanced to the stage in her so-called military career after basic training. That required Star Soldiers to go outside on mock patrol missions, for long periods that required them to perform bivouacs and other forms of outdoor camping. So Jefferson never would have encountered the lesbian Soldiers who actively recruited "sidekicks"- i.e. sexual partners- to share their sleeping bags- and the related amenities- overnight. Abruptly, she made a move to apologize to Jefferson with a quick embrace.

"I'm sorry, Jeff," Hamilton said. "Gosh, I am *so* sorry. I completely misinterpreted what you said, and I really took it the wrong way. Can you forgive me?"

"Sure," said Jefferson, with a nod. "What did you think I meant?"

Hamilton proceeded to explain the custom that created such distaste for the word "sidekick" in her mind, before Jefferson abruptly told her to stop.

"That's not what I had in mind," she said. "*At all.* I have enough trouble trying to keep track of which *boys* I've made out with- and there's been a *lot*- to start adding *girls* to that list. And I *do* remember you getting propped by some of the bolder girls in camp during basic, by the way- they never did that to me, since I was still pretty damn ugly then- and thinking it was...well....odd. I don't mind it if they decide to live their way like that- just don't try to get *me* into it."

"That's how I felt, too."

"Anyway, "sidekick" is kind of a dated term for what the job I was thinking of implies- without the sexual bit, I mean. It might be better to say that you'd be my "friend", but you were that before, so we couldn't necessary use that. So... "

"I'm starting to get what you want. You want a companion for when you go off adventuring, and so on?"

"Yeah. The "and so on" would be being my partner. In *business*, of course."

"Of course."

"I've been around a bit, and I know some things about how this wide universe operates, but not absolutely everywhere. You've probably been places I've never been before, and know some things I don't know about. The Star Soldiers have to be everything to everybody, so you probably picked more than a few things that'd be useful to a freebooter like me who's never been or worked in the places you've been and I haven't."

"Perfectly. Not that it matters, but how would I get....?"

"Same as I do. But we'll split it down the middle. That's the only fair way to do this. Especially when your partner is also your best buddy."

"Then I'm in....*buddy*," Hamilton concluded, as they shook paws on the deal.

III.

Having successfully renewed their friendship, Jefferson and Hamilton walked to Jefferson's aforementioned apartment building, located at the corner of Asimov Avenue and Pohl Street, in a largely working class district of the city. As she promised, Jefferson vouched for Hamilton's character as a potential tenant. But it wasn't so much Jefferson's friendship as much as the fact that Hamilton was a decorated and wounded ex-Star Soldier- a military tradition ran deep in the landlord's family- and had a reliable and dependable source of income- unlike most of the other tenants of the building- that secured Hamilton's possession of the apartment directly beneath Jefferson's. It was another sign that the onceclose relationship between them was going to resume, almost as if nothing had happened in the interim.

They celebrated in the manner they had developed for such a thing during their leaves in basic training- which was drinking. Alcohol. Definitely more than one drink, each.

In the old days, Hamilton, despite her smaller size, had been the one who handled her liquor better. Jefferson had been more likely to pass out after only two drinks, or even one and a half. However, the circumstances had been changed with the super-canine abilities Jefferson now possessed. Jefferson now was capable of drinking as much as possible, as quickly as possible, and Hamilton struggled to keep up. They were equally affected by the beer, but, as soon as they started taking drops of the harder stuff, the difference became much more noticeable. It took Jefferson until her fifth whisky to realize that Hamilton had passed out about three drinks before. At which point, after settling the bill by putting it on her "tab", she lifted her smaller colleague on her torso, piggy-back style, dragged her home, tucked into the bedroom of her new apartment, and then went to bed herself in the room above.

*

For the first time in a long time, not having to abide by the incessant choruses of Taps and Reveille on a regular basis, Hamilton slept well. The drunken stupor she fell into contributed to that, but it was also due to the fact that her circadian rhythms had been strongly compromised by anxiety that had built up constantly during the time of her Court Martial and after her discharge. She had been worried about not having anything permanent to rely on now she had been cut off from daily duties in the Star Soldiers. Now that was all a thing of the past, and, with a new job and residence, she could establish something at least close to way she had once lived before the Soldiers came into her life.

Or so she thought.

It was only a few hours into the new morning when Hamilton found herself suddenly awoken with a pail of water thrown into her face, which jolted her upright immediately.

Inevitably, it was Jefferson who had done the deed.

Only showing a slight remnant of the consequences of last night, in comparison with Hamilton, she was dressed in her regular clothing, standing above the still prone Hamilton, anxiously stamping her foot on the ground.

When Hamilton recovered her wits and nerve, she was not only fully conscious, but also angry. She'd punished underlings in the Star Soldiers for doing that kind of "fooling around" regularly as an officer.

This line of activity, in her mind, seemed simply as aspect of that, and nothing else.

"What," she demanded of her friend, "was *that* for?"

"I needed to get you up," Jefferson explained. "And, if you're hearing is as compromised as your vision..."

"It *isn't*," retorted Hamilton. "You could've just whispered in my ear, and I would have gotten your point easily. No need for getting me *wet* while you did it."

"Oh. Well, my *point* in doing that, as you said, was that you needed to be woken up. And that-...," she gestured to the bucket, now returned to the floor, "seemed like the only solution. You were still in residence in Dreamland pretty deeply."

"And just, for what reason, was I supposed to be woken up at....let's see here...", said Hamilton, looking at her watch on the bedside table, and then goggling her eyes in shock. "*FIVE* AM?" Jefferson shushed her, and then they resumed talking in softer tones.

"The "reason"," Jefferson resumed, "is that I- or should I say, *we-* have a job to do. But if you're going to be acting so high and mighty with me, just because you got woken up at a time that you don't believe that an officer of the God all mighty Star Soldiers should be civilly woken up at, maybe you aren't as suited to enduring the sorts of deprivations that go along with my gig all the time as I thought you were, and, therefore, you can't handle the risks and consequences of...."

"No," Hamilton answered, contritely. "I'm sorry. I still have the Star Soldiers inside of me. When I went out in bivouacs with the younger kids, as I was often *required* to do, there were quite a few who liked to pull that kind of stunt on the officers they weren't very fond of as some sort of "joke". Or things that were even worse than that. I punished people severely for less than that, Jeff. Very strictly, and without any sort of compassion. Because that ridiculous kind of "humor" wasn't "funny" then, and it still isn't now."

"I wasn't trying to do it as a joke, Ham. That was the last thing on my mind. This was born out of necessity..."

"Of course it was, Jeff. That I totally got. You could have done less extravagant sorts of things than that to wake me up, though. That way I wouldn't have gotten so sore at you for being woken up so soon.

Anyway, what happened after that was all my fault, for overreacting. I need to learn how to loosen up more, now that I'm not a Soldier. You're gonna help me with that, right?" "Will I *ever*," Jefferson leered, very knowingly.

"Just get out of here and let me get dressed," answered Hamilton, not liking what Jefferson's leer seemed to be implying in her eyes. "You know I don't like people looking at me while I dress." "Of course," said Jefferson, withdrawing respectfully from the room.

*

Once Hamilton was outfitted in her normal civilian clothes, they left the apartment house and proceeded north on Pohl. This was a very shady neighborhood, but the duo managed to walk unescorted through it for blocks without being threatened by any actual or potential violence. Hamilton seemed to guess that Jefferson's substantial celebrity, coupled with an awestruck kind of fear that the legendary status of her powers instilled in many members of the community, was responsible for this. The residents seemed to be whispering her name in each other's ears everywhere they went, and giving the duo a wide berth on the sidewalk as they meandered. Hamilton was struck with the fact that Jefferson was so easily recognized and known. Nobody, in contrast, recognized *her*- though she suspected that, the longer she became associated with Jefferson, this would change.

"You have more....admirers...than I figured," Hamilton mused.

"It's just my reputation preceding me, as usual," said Jefferson. "You beat up one person, or one person's evil army, or one person's evil army of robot killers, and then you never hear the end of it. But I don't do that on a daily basis, and certainly not to people who don't deserve it. Besides: I spent my whole childhood and youth growing up here, the same as a lot of the members of my family did. So, if the people here don't know me, they've at least heard of me. Even if it's just through that ridiculous way the media glorifies everything I do."

"I don't really know a whole lot about what you've been doing, Jefferson. I was off Earth for quite a while before I came back, remember? And the few sources of media I was allowed access to in the

Soldiers were pretty heavily censored. "Morale" reasons, mostly, was what they said it was all about. So I'm not sure about how I fit in..."

"It's not that hard. You'll get the hang of it once we're off doing the assignment."

"And when will *that* be? Seems like we've been walking for hours. I don't know about you, but I need a coffee. Bad! If only there was some sort of…"

"It's being provided at the meeting, by our client."

"But where is the place where we're supposed…"

"Right there. Come on. If we hurry, we can just avoid being late."

Unconsciously, Jefferson grabbed Hamilton's paw, and dragged her inside to the place where they were supposed to meet the being who would tell them what they were assigned to do.

*

The building was typical of the city, predating the era of its current residents by a long amount of time, as it had been erected back when the humans were still alive. It had previously been the main downtown branch of a fairly prosperous bank, and the exterior showed it. It was constructed entirely of a still-gleaming white marble, with high columns in the Doric style guarding the front entrance. Out at the front was a bronze statue of a lone human soldier, meant to represent the victims of a long ago and completely forgotten war of the past. The main building itself would have stood out as a classic representation of the city's prior prosperity- were it not for the fact that it was forcibly attached to a higher and uglier looking skyscraper which had obviously been erected at a much later date.

The interior was much the same, the current landlord having felt things were all right as they were, design wise, and did not need to be altered much to conform to any contemporary architectural trends. Besides, the building's original purpose was much in the same department as its current owner's line of work. His job also involved the usage and handling of money, although it was in a much more illegal vein than that of a legitimate financial institution.

As instructed, Jefferson and Hamilton went and sat in the front lobby, where they were able to refresh themselves with coffee and food that seemed to have been specially provided for them. This they did largely in silence. Unlike its prior days of prosperity, the former bank now rarely got visitors- well in keeping with its current reputation in this now disreputable neighborhood.

Presently, the current owner, who was much responsible for the bad reputation the place currently held, made himself known.

D.T. Poodle was formidable a figure financially as Jefferson Ball was physically. Despite the fact that he had run through more than one fortune in his lifetime, he apparently had enough money stashed away to allow him not only to continue to fund an opulent lifestyle, but also to fund serious political ambitions, which worried those who felt he was not at all "there" inside his head should he, somehow and someway, rise to a position of considerable social and political influence. He was the object of considerable mockery, particularly because he had, in a moment of rashness in his youth, dyed the upper part of his white pelt bright red, which gave him the appearance forever after of a somewhat belligerent rooster. Although the red had faded into a mellower orange over time, the belligerency had not faded. D.T. was well known for his generosity towards friends and acquaintances, but was starkly mean and obsessive towards enemies. This befitted the image of the "gangster" he was often accused of being, although it was an image that he, seeking to be, and attempting to act as, a more "refined" being, repeatedly and harshly disowned. That did not, however, mean that the image had no truth behind it.

Jefferson had the good fortune to be considered one of D.T.'s "friends", and his manner upon greeting her showed it, when he blew her a "kiss" in the air. Hamilton, however, aroused his suspicion.

"She with you?" he demanded of Jefferson, in a very nasal and very brusque working class accent.

"Yeah," she answered, in the same sort of speech. "Major Pomeranian..." (Hamilton saluted, as if on auto pilot from her old days) "...is an old acquaintance of mine. You know how I used to be in the Star Soldiers- or *tried* to be, at any rate? She was my friend, and she made it- very well, too- there. Well, she got wounded, and, because they don't truck with weakness, they dumped her. I ran into her the other day nearly getting rolled, and rescued her. She doesn't have a lot of other prospects right now, so I decided to take her on as my s......"

At the near-mention of the word "sidekick", Hamilton glared viciously at Jefferson. Abruptly, Jefferson knew she had to use a better synonym in place of that word.

"...business partner," continued Jefferson, as Hamilton went at ease. "So, from now on, when you're dealing with me, you're dealing with her also, whether you like it or not."

"Any *objections*?" interjected Hamilton, to make sure of the fact that she hadn't been roused from her sleep so early in the day for "nothing".

"No," said D.T. "Of course not. The Star Soldiers always do jobs tightly and efficiently, whatever it is. I only wish *my* people had that kind of discipline. You'd be bringing a lot to the table to Jefferson's operation, Major, hopefully in a *positive* way."

The emphasized word in the last spoken sentence was aimed at Jefferson, who winced. Evidently, despite her fabled abilities, she wasn't able to complete "assignments" to D.T.'s satisfaction every single time he gave them to her. Hamilton got the hint.

"I'm sure I can put some discipline into her, sir," she said. "Although she's been trying her best to make me *less* disciplined every day."

That was meant to be a joke, and was accepted as such, with the three of them laughing. Then, they shifted to the business that had called the ladies there.

"So what's the matter this time, D.T.?" Jefferson asked.

"The usual," he answered, without bothering to provide any information more specific than that.

Jefferson nodded, as she understood exactly what he meant. It almost seemed as if the gathering were going to break up early, since D.T. appeared to give Jefferson information that would be privy only to her and to be revealed to no one else. Hamilton, however, was not to be left out.

"What do you mean, "the usual"?" she said.

D.T., not expecting this complication, curled his lips up in a threatening pose, but Jefferson glared back at him silently, as if she were telling him that she would explain everything to Hamilton, without any needless complications. Which she then set out to do.

"Hamilton," Jefferson asked, "did you, at any time, have to do guard duty on a spaceship that was carrying a shipment from the Treasury?"

"Yeah," answered Hamilton. "More than once. It was a requirement. The idea was that we were supposed to prove that we had no avarice in our bones, and that we were supposed to prove how "loyal" we were by getting the money to where it was meant to go without any problems. Not exactly pleasant, what with the threat being robbed hanging over things all the time, but it had to be done."

"Well, this is kind of like that," said Jefferson. "Only we aren't so much as taking money from a place so that it can be stored away in some vault, as we are relieving it from someone and bringing it back."

"Specifically," added D.T., "someone who *owes* me that some of money, and has, for unknown and undisclosed reasons, failed to pay it back."

"I see," said Hamilton, catching on. "So you...?"

"....lent him or her that money," finished D.T. "That's how I make my living. I get approached by people who need that money, and I give it to them. Like if they need it to pay their rent, or something really important or significant like that. Jefferson herself here has partaken of this service more than a few times..."

Jefferson silently mouthed profanity at him.

"...so she knows the consequences of *not* paying me back," he concluded.

"Let me get this straight," Hamilton said. "You give these people money, free of charge, and they either pay you back or they don't. Why should they be punished if they don't pay you back? Surely you have enough left to be able to finance your... ventures...without that money magically appearing on your ledger overnight, don't you?"

"That's...not how it works, Ham," Jefferson responded, with a growing nervousness her friend could not have failed to pick up on.

"Yeah," D.T. added. "I don't "give" it to them "free of charge". You may be an experienced soldier,

Major, but, if I may say so, you don't seem to understand how business really works. At the very least, you don't understand how *my* business works. Which is as follows. I give them the money, yes. But they have to pay it back to me, whenever they can. With *interest* accrued, of course."

It was then Hamilton saw what she and Jefferson had gotten involved in. She trembled with rage, for she had not signed on for anything resembling this at all.

"*Interest?*" she spat.

"Of course, interest," D.T. continued, calmly. "That's the only way you make any *profits* on this gig. If you don't understand what that means..."

"I *do*," Hamilton growled. "It means you're a lousy, rotten little...."

"...it *means*," said D.T., ignoring her entirely, "that a certain percentage of the total amount is tacked on the sum I have loaned the person for each day that they do not reimburse me. And the percentage increases at the whim of the person loaning the sum, and can, if they are not like *me,* become enormously high. Some of my competitors- whom *you* must be thinking of, Major- put high numbers up for their rates from the start. 100%, 200%, 300%, that sort of thing.

"But I'm *different*. I'm more *honest*. I don't spring the fact that the interest is being added on after I've loaned them the money and they've blown it, like some of them do. I explain it to my clients clearly and directly, without none of that fancy lawyer talk. *Or* the loud-mouthed hysteria with which the dumb, stupid and out of touch media's always tainting my job with. I say, "I can give you the $100, sure, but you know you got to pay me back for it, don't you?" And they say, "Yeah." And I say, "Here's how it is.

For every day you *don't* pay me, I add a percentage to the total. You know how 1% of $100 is $1, right? Well, the first day after you don't pay me at the agreed time, you will owe me $101 instead of $100. And then, the day *after* that, we add 2% of $100, which is $2. That's $103." And so on and so on, until the bum get wise and pays.

"But some of 'em never understand that, and fly off this here Earth *without* ever paying me back, and *then* I got to resort to extreme measures. Like hiring you and your friend here to find 'em and *force* 'em to pay me back!"

"*But*," Hamilton interjected, carefully controlling her rage as a veteran Soldier would, "they must have good reasons for not paying back. Like, maybe, the fact that the rates you charge make it *impossible* for them to pay you back!"

Jefferson gasped at this break of the usual protocol and gaped at Hamilton for saying what she said. This was something that was simply not done around D.T., for fear of igniting his hair trigger temper. Hamilton, however, was unmoved. She knew nothing of his reputation, so she had nothing to fear from him. He was, in her mind, just another one of the young punks who annoyed and tested her as a Star Soldier, and she intended to treat him as such.

D.T., fortunately for them both, kept his temper.

"What you *don't* understand about all this, Major," he said, "is that most of the people I work with make wages that are barely allow them to survive, owing to the cost of living. Coupled with the fact that our political class is so insensitive that they barely *acknowledge* the presence of my clients in society, let alone give them the kind of supplements to their income that could benefit them. And those beings I treat with the greatest of kindness. I may not look like it now, but I grew up in the same kind of circumstances as they did, and I can sympathize with their plight easily because of that. Anyone who was in their situation can. Just ask your friend here. She came out of the bottom same as I did.

"What I am asking you and her to do, however, has nothing to do with that. This is about collecting something that is *due* to me which has not been given back, because the perpetrator no longer resides on Earth, and I cannot track him down myself. I may appear healthy, but I have weak lungs that prevent me from breathing anything but the air of Earth. On the other hand, you two have been in space before and have adapted to it. Thus, the reason why you have been deputized by me.

"The person who is the subject of your hunt is an old friend of mine from the past. Once upon a time, it may surprise you to learn, I had a strong taste for a variety of disreputable pursuits, gambling being key among them. Well, this fellow kept it up after I had given it up, and he has forever been borrowing sums from me without either the ability or the desire to pay it back. I kept a running record of how much he owes me with the growing interest tacked on, just as I would any other deadbeat who can't or won't pay. And I find now that he owes me the not insubstantial sum of $10,000. *But,* as I implied earlier, he has now mysteriously relocated off-planet, so I cannot find him, catch him, or force him to repay said sum myself. You, however, are in the perfect position to do this *for* me.

"You will not, however, be doing this unrewarded. I will, of course, be underwriting the costs of your transportation to and from entirely, so that your undernourished wallets will not leave you flat broke, what with the costs of renting private spaceships these days. In addition, I will, as I usually do, be offering you a percentage of the collected sum once it is collected and brought back to me. I think a 25% share of the total would be fair enough, wouldn't it?"

Before Hamilton could say anything further, Jefferson nodded, implicitly agreeing to the deal as it stood. She wasn't going to risk having her "partner" jeopardize this potentially lucrative deal as it stood now, despite Hamilton's inquisitiveness into things that should have remained a mystery to her. This was emphasized by the sour glare she made towards Hamilton just after that.

"Good," said D.T., closing the deal. "I will e-mail you the further details about the bastard for whom you are hunting, along with the details about where to find your private ship and where to bring it when you complete the mission in the agreed-upon time. Thank you for your service."

Without another word, he turned his back on Jefferson and Hamilton, and exited the room with a soldier-like step reminiscent of Hamilton herself in her prime.

*

After they finished their visit to D.T., Jefferson and Hamilton prepared to return back to the apartments. Or at least, Jefferson did. Hamilton, in a show of defiance, chose to stand where she was, not moving an inch. When Jefferson discovered Hamilton was not following her back, she went back towards the smaller dog, and tried to force her into pounding the pavement.

Despite Jefferson's best efforts, Hamilton would not move. Neither gentle coaxing, nor shouting in her ear, nor threats of being severely and strongly punched and/or kicked, nor a detailed description of how and where she would be bitten upon her person if she did not comply with Jefferson's demands *immediately,* would deter Hamilton from completing her appointed rounds. Finally, when Jefferson grabbed one of her arms and tried to drag her back just as she had dragged her into the bank, Hamilton responded. She shirked out of Jefferson's grasp and resumed her vigil. That was when Jefferson finally lost what little limited patience remained inside of her immortal soul.

"What in the hell is the *matter* with you?" she shouted. "It can't be something *I* did, because, as I recall,

I've treated you with the utmost *kindness* since you were…"

"It *was* something you did!" Hamilton shot back. "Something not very *ethical*."

"Oh, it *was,* huh?" Jefferson fired back. "And what was *that*?"

"You're fully aware of what it was. You agreed to his damned *deal* without *consulting* me on it *whatsoever*."

"I've worked with him before, and I know how he works. There was no need for you to horn in on it. You don't know him the same way I do. Hell, you almost botched things with that damned loose and suspicious tongue of yours! He doesn't like being quizzed about what he does, and he's never gonna look at me the same way now that you've stuck your little nose into his business more than is good for either of us! I'm *sorry* if you don't think him pleasant company, but that's his way. You have to adapt to what the contractor wants, or you don't get paid. That's the first rule of this business, and you should damn well know it if you don't by now!"

"And that, apparently, is all YOU *care* about!"

"Just *what* are you implying?"

"That you're doing "*business*" with a slime-ball LOAN SHARK! And you don't seem to notice and even

CARE that he *is* one in the first place!"

"And exactly *who* should I be doing business with, may I ask? How many *ethical* people are there in his kind of business? Or *any* kind of business, for that matter? You know the answer the same as I do, Hamilton."

Hamilton sighed.

"Look," she said, in a calmer voice, "you call yourself a "heroine". A "super heroine", even."

"Call? I am! *Cogito ergo sum,* remember?"

"That's not the philosopher I'd quote here. This has a lot more to do with Aristotle."

"How so?"

"Your *ethics,* you *moron*!" Hamilton spat, as her rage returned.

"Ethics? What has *that* got to do with....?"

"If you're a heroine," Hamilton interrupted, "you're supposed to be representing the side of the good. That means you only interact with evil to *destroy* it. You *certainly* don't interact with it on a regular basis in terms of *business* propositions!"

"I see," said Jefferson. "You think D.T. is evil. But he clearly said that he..."

"His kind of being will do *anything* to keep up a front," said Hamilton. "That goes with everything his kind says or does, at any time, in any place. If he has to lie, steal, cheat or kill to keep up his position in life, he'll do it. Never mind if anyone "good" is in his way if he does it- and never mind if they don't get *hurt* in the process!"

"Is that you talking," Jefferson snapped, "or the *Star Soldiers*?"

"Both," retorted Hamilton. "Do you know how many of those kind of jerks I had to stare down and lecture about morals, particularly their *lack* of such, all over the galaxy? They weren't sending me to those places for some sort of pleasure cruise, Jefferson. Oh, most certainly NOT. Our reason for being there was all about maintaining the law and order I was trained to maintain, and I did it. That's the Star Soldier in me reacting to this. But there's another aspect to this whole affair that's personal to me. *Much* more personal."

"What was it?" Jefferson inquired softly, sensing, correctly, that this was something that needed to be broached with sensitivity.

"I never told you this before," said Hamilton. "But I have a complete and total apathy towards everything that Poodle fellow and his "job" stand for. There's a good reason for it, of course. You know that I came from what appeared to you be a "better" neighborhood than yours. Well, that only tells you so much about me. Yeah, my dad had a good job and he provided well for us- but only up to a point.

Eventually, though, he wasn't able to make ends meet like he should. He couldn't get a raise for the life of him, the way the company he worked for was run, and he went out and got a loan. That would have been all right if he'd gone to a legitimate bank, and got a loan on reasonable terms. But he ended up going to one of those awful "payday loan" companies that D.T. was implying were his "competition".

"And what happened? He wasn't able to pay the loan back?"

"That's the simplest way of putting it. He hadn't read the fine print about the loan when he signed the papers for it, and we only discovered, too late, that he had to pay *300%* interest. On *every day* he didn't pay!

"You can guess what happened right away. We were ruined financially. Dad and Mom swore they would work to pay things back, and I volunteered to work as well to drop the size of the numbers. But nothing worked. I'm pretty sure that's what killed both of them- stress, and overwork. It nearly drove me down the bend, too.

"But I escaped from that stress- and conquered it, for the most part- by joining the Star Soldiers. I sure as hell couldn't go to college after I left high school, not with the debts my family owed, and they offered me such a nice chance for me to have a decent, honorable career. Along with a chance to show people, especially all those crumbs who thought my life and I weren't worth much, that I was doing something with some value. And I guess I did some good being in there. I don't know that for sure, yet. But you never forget being a tough financial spot, Jefferson. So, if I *offended* you by showing your high hatted money lender friend some justified *contempt*, I'm sorry. As you know now, I have a perfectly good reason for it. I hope you can..."

"I can," finished Jefferson. "Wow! Trust me to enter into working for somebody who represents the same bunch that ruined your life. If I'd only known that before I started doing jobs for him..."

"Now you do," answered Hamilton.

"But I'll tell you one thing I know for sure I'm gonna do now. All this time, I was thinking about using D.T. to resolve my own financial problems, and not about how that made people see me for using his services. Of course, I had to. Most of the time, I don't make money regularly, and I got overhead- i.e. my arm and leg sum of rent- that *has* to be paid regularly. So he was my only option when I was short. I mean, he was willing to forgive some of what I owed him because I look good and have super powers and a glamorous job and all that, but that only goes so far. This was all before I met you. You'd be willing to lend me cash if I needed it, wouldn't you?"

"Sure. That's what friends are for, aren't they? And I wouldn't charge you "interest" for it, by any means.

I know better than that."

"I should, too. And I think I will. As you said, I should be more concerned about my ethics, and setting out the best image I can as a fighter for the "good" and all that if I want people to trust me in their best interests. Well, if I'm doing that, why am I dealing with an extortionist who uses the money he collects for who knows what evil thing?"

"Exactly."

"Then- after we fulfill this contract, of course-I'm cutting him off. I'm not going to use his services, or do any more "jobs" for him, or anything like that anymore. Besides, my share of the collection fee should leave me all right financially- for the time being."

"It hopefully *should*."

"Okay. Will you come back to the apartment, now? We should be getting the information about the guy pretty soon on the computer."
"Yes. I think I will."

And they walked back, both with a clear sense of satisfaction and catharsis in their hearts.

IV.

Jefferson was correct about the information having arrived on the computer, by the time they made it back to the apartments. The biggest surprise, however, was learning who they were supposed to catch.

Jefferson signalled this with a loud gasp, which brought Hamilton over to her side.

"You see this?" said Jefferson, gesturing to the monitor. "The past never goes away. It just keeps coming back on you like a bad penny."

"Uh huh," answered Hamilton. "That is definitely a name that is familiar to us both."

"Definitely. That bastard was responsible for me losing my virginity. Back when I was ugly, I mean. Said it was a "favor" to me, owing to the fact that nobody would "have" me otherwise. True back then at least, but surely not now."

"He said the same thing to *me* when he took *mine*."

"*What*?" This was news to Jefferson, who didn't think Hamilton shared her taste in boys at all.

"Sure. He dipped his pen in any available ink then. Probably still does, wherever he is now."

"What ever happened to him?"

"Oh, they bounced him from the unit just after you got tossed."

"What for?"

"Gambling. A bigger addiction for him than sex, even. Got into such big debts that he owed the whole force, and no one would cover his losses anymore. So he just left one day without a word of warning, and never squared or owned up for any of the pennies he'd taken."

"Typical. Well, it's no surprise he'd get in with D.T., then. *Or* that he'd end up owing him ten grand." "Does he give us any reasonable clues where he may be?"

"Seems like he's over in the Jones-Maltese quadrant of District Five. You know, over by the border between Milky Way and Andromeda."

Hamilton scratched the top of her hat-covered head with a paw.

"I don't think I've ever had the pleasure of being out in that part of the galaxy," she said. "You know anything about it?"

"Sure," said Jefferson. "Pretty nasty place. There wasn't anything there a little while ago, so you probably weren't sent to patrol it on account of that. But then, some desperate prospector got marooned on some little Oort cloud or other, and he found some precious metals there, and..."

"I can guess," Hamilton concluded, paws on hips. "A lawless place, with more respect for a person based on how they can fight or shoot, rather on their intelligence. And all of them fighting for control of a single and precious vital resource, without which the place would lose its economic and population base."

"Huh?"

"Why everyone's *there* in the first place, silly."

"Gotcha. Well, it seemed like that the last time I was there, anyway. The men are tough, the women are tougher, and the *kids* are even tougher than *that*."

"Who would want to bring up *kids* in *that* kind of place?"

"Beats me."

"Anyway, that's none of our business. What *we* need to be concerned about is *defending* ourselves out there. From *any* possible threat."

"Please. I can acquit myself well in a fist fight. Haven't been bested yet."

"That's not what I meant. When I was discharged, they took away my gun."

"And so?"

"Unlike *you*, I don't have any super canine abilities. And I'm not exactly a *giant*, either. If some tankedup loser tries to do the same thing to me that old Jackpot Dingo did to me *and* you a long time ago, *without* my consent, I'm gonna need some way of threatening him off. By potentially being able to poison him with lead, if you catch my drift."

"Right."

"So where might one find a piece here?"

"In this neighborhood, the best bet is to hit one of the pawn shops. Most of the high rollers give their weapons in for cash when they need it."

"Would they have one of my old Star Soldier guns? Sometimes, if the grunts were in that kind of position, they'd pawn their guns to get some cash. Against regulations, of course. But you know how desperate some people can get."

"Go ahead. You might get lucky, and get one for a fraction of the amount it cost the Star Soldiers to fit you out with it in the first place."

"I sure hope so." Hamilton walked to the door, but then turned around. "Pension notwithstanding, I'm not made of money." She glared in no nonsense fashion at her friend, with a very large undercurrent of friendly but still unmistakable menace. "*Remember that.*"

Jefferson grinned sheepishly. Hamilton couldn't tell whether or not she was sincere, or just faking it.

*

Hamilton did, indeed, "get lucky". As it happens, there were quite a number of choice weapons available at the nearest pawn shop. And a number of them were guns owned by current and former ex-Star Soldiers. So many, in fact, that the owner was now having a cut rate 2-for-1 sale. Hamilton was able to get a barely used one for herself- and another for Jefferson, just in case- at a mere fraction of the cost that she had predicted she might have to spend, which pleased her considerably.

Then it was time for them to pick up the "rig" that had been assigned to them by their temporary employer, and go off to do the job as planned.

The ship was one of the kind that, since the canine race of Earth had made contact with the alien races beyond, had been produced on a mass level, not unlike cars once upon a time, for mass usage. Efficiently and economically built, they were constructed on fuel sources dependent on advanced chemistry and physics rather than natural Earth resources, and at their highest speeds, could conquer high distances very easily. They had made it fairly easy for a wide swatch of the galaxy to come under either the direct control or the economic influence of Earth, which necessitated, among other things, the continued presence of the Star Soldiers in the various spheres of the galaxy that required Earth's involvement.

Yet overproduction had, again as with cars, created a caste system among the vehicles. The ones produced most recently were at the top, as they were the most expensive, and, therefore, the least used and in the best working condition. Then came the middle ground, the barely used or still in good working order models that had been off-loaded in favor of a pristine new one. At the bottom were the over-used, dinged up or barely functioning models, the ones made first, and most imperfectly, among the earliest class of ships, and the ones discarded almost immediately when superior models replaced them. Yet these models were, miraculously, still able to work, which made them the ideal source for use by people with very limited means.

Guess which kind Jefferson and Hamilton had been assigned.

"*Really*?" said Jefferson, indignantly, when she saw the ship for the first time.

"Oh, come on, Jeff," said Hamilton. "Don't take it personal. It can get us there and back, at least, by the looks of it. Well, maybe just there. Isn't that what we want?"

"I suppose. But D.T.'s being a real penny pincher this time out. If he cared at all about us, he would have let us have a better one that's more suitable to beings of our reps."

"You know perfectly well that it isn't his way to "care" about anybody. If he actually "cared" about the welfare of his clients, he wouldn't be in the money lending business at all, and we wouldn't be doing this in the first place. *Or* making the money from it. So suck it up."

"All right. But I'm driving."

"You got the training to handle it?" Hamilton raised an eyebrow as she spoke.

"Yeah," Jefferson scoffed. "Why *wouldn't* I have it?"

This was not the truth. The truth revealed itself when Jefferson, after adjusting the ship into vertical take off position, pulled the wrong one of the several dozen levers available on the consoles to the right and in front of the driver's seat, and sent the ship backwards several feet into the ground.

"Oops," she said, joshing. "Had the silly thing in reverse." But Hamilton wasn't laughing.

"You can't drive one of these things *at all, can* you?" she snapped, demanding the truth.

"Well, I didn't end up finishing the correspondence course, but I can still..."

"*Correspondence* course? For flying a *spaceship*?" Hamilton growled. "That's the most ridiculous idea ever conceived! You can't learn how to fly a ship if nobody's there to guide you through it."

"And I suppose *you* could do it better?"

"*I* actually *attended* the lectures on how to operate a spaceship when they were *offered* to me."

"It's not my fault that I got thrown out before then. I've been trying ever since to catch up..."

Hamilton stopped Jefferson from talking by holding her paw over Jefferson's mouth, as Jefferson herself had already done to her several times before.

"Listen, *heroine*," she said. "I can understand you running around the universe in your short pants, making love to half the universe and fighting the other half, and talking big about what you can do, like some old timey pro wrestler. Somehow, you managed to get all the rubes out there to buy whatever fanciful stories you invented about yourself. Particularly the ones that have you at your most "heroic". But I want you to know something here and now. You're dealing with the one person in the whole universe that you *can't* fool. None of your overstated, feminism inflated B.S. will work with me. Dig? I may not be as famous, or as celebrated, or as gosh darned *physically attractive* as you, but I've been around. I've seen and heard the same damned things as you, and been in the same sort of situations as you. Not as often, mind you, but I've been there. So trying to treat me as an inferior, however unintentional it might be, will not work here.

"And let's not forget the one crucial thing in all of this. *I knew you when.* And I'm perfectly willing and able to explain who the "real" Jefferson Ball was, and *is,* should I be asked. All you need to do for *that* to happen would be to push me far enough to make me want to spill to the Internet, and then you'd be *finished.* So keep *that* in mind when you try to treat me like one of your moronic "admirers"."

She released Jefferson from her grip, much stronger than it appeared to be.

"Ham, you wouldn't do that to me!" said Jefferson, in horror. "I spent so much time developing my image. And my *reputation.* All the time you were building the career in the Star Soldiers that I lost out on, I was building my image as a ball busting fighter. And *lover.* You have no idea what I put myself through to build that image. Or what it *cost* me, besides. There might be a lot of talk about me that's exaggeration, and I won't deny I played a role in spreading that bunk myself. But there's also a lot that's perfectly *true.* That I really worked and slaved for in order to build. You don't know what that means to me. After all the time I grew up being ignored and dismissed when I was a kid, you can't understand what it means to me to actually be able to live the life I dreamed about and be able to do the things I dreamed about *now.* Please don't take that away from me. *Please.*"

"Calm down, *drama queen,*" said Hamilton. "I didn't say I was going to give away anything about you. What kind of greedy, insensitive ingrate do you think I am? All I was implying by saying all that was that, because you're so used to being a solo act, you haven't entirely learned how to think about other people-i.e. me- as your equals. But, as we agreed only recently, you are now in a *partnership* with me, and we need to think of ourselves as such. That means no B.S., no fibbing, and no grandstanding of any kind with me. I don't mind if you do it with others, but *respect* me and my *intelligence. Understand?*" Jefferson nodded.

"Good," concluded Hamilton, undoing her seat belt. "Now get out of that seat and let me handle this thing."

V.

Those who invented and perfected the automobile in the late 19th and early 20th centuries believed they were doing a wealth of good to the people of Earth, but they also could not have foreseen the economic, emotional, and environmental destruction their descendants would ultimately unleash through the invention in the years following their deaths. This was, likewise, with the long ago canines who had taken the human invention of the spaceship and made it not only an efficient and practical form of transportation, but one affordable to anyone in the galaxy who wanted one. And so, just as the lush green hills and valleys of Earth were now disfigured by seemingly endless loops of gravel and asphalt meant to take automobiles from one near or far place to another, so the once barren loneliness of space was suddenly clogged with traffic needing to- and able- to cross entire groups of light years on a daily basis. That is, when dozens of other vehicles were *not* trying to do the same thing at the same time.

Jefferson and Hamilton met this with the typical responses of motorists past to such tie ups. Hamilton, with the dispassion her military career had imposed upon her, circled calmly into and around various bottlenecks, and waited with the same patience when there were lines or accidents holding things up. Jefferson, however, displayed the legacies of the limited amount of experience she had gotten behind the wheel in the past in her behavior. More than once, to Hamilton's displeasure, she cheered their getting through past other drivers by "flipping" them "the bird", or gestured and spoke profanely to them when, in her minds, they were "cut off" in a blatantly unfair fashion. Hamilton was able to bear this for a while, but, when it had happened more times than her patience could bear, she turned her head, and glared at Jefferson like a parent pushed too far by a child.

"*Stop that*!" she ordered.

"I'm only giving them what they deserve," retorted Jefferson.

"*You* deserve not to be travelling this way, if you can't handle it."

"Oh, treat me like one of your grunts, will ya? This isn't the same thing as…"

"Yes, it is. If I spoke to them like that, it was because they weren't acting as ordered. *Or* if they were being *immature*. Like *you* are, *now*."

"Then *they're* being immature…"

"Never *mind* them! The way you gain *respect* from people, Jefferson, is by *not* stooping to their level. If you conduct yourself responsibly, and show yourself *worthy* of respect, then you'll get it."

"Hamilton, don't assume that everyone is able to "conduct" themselves as "responsibly" as you! Because I know for a fact that there are very few people like that. Especially here in this uncivilized place."

"All the more reason for us to behave. Uncivilized places only become civilized ones if civilization is brought to them by people who are *already* civilized."

"Just like a Star Soldier to say that. What'd you do, quote from the conduct manual or something?"

Abruptly, Hamilton put on the anti-gravity brakes of the car, and it was put in idle mode, stranding its occupants in the barren blackness. She then pulled her gun out, according to old habits, and aimed at Jefferson.

"You," she warned her friend, "can get out and *walk* back to Earth if you're going to keep speaking like that to me! And, if you *keep* doing it, I'll shoot you in the right places, and you can have the same *disabilities* I now have. Then we'll be *even*. How about *that*?"

"You wish," taunted Jefferson. "You might have been a good shot when you had both eyes, but I doubt you'd be able to hit me now. Besides, me having super powers and all, you'd just be wasting a...."

Hamilton shot at Jefferson's right boot, barely missing her foot. Outraged, Jefferson removed her seat belt and leaned over the side to get at Hamilton. She grabbed the ex-Star Soldier fiercely around her chest with both paws, her own large chest threatening to pin Hamilton down. Hamilton retorted by breaking Jefferson's hold on her, and hitting her in the face with the paw that wasn't holding the gun.

Jefferson lunged for the gun, grabbed it out of Hamilton's paws, and took a shot at her. In doing so, she missed by a wide margin, but ended up hitting the control console of the ship, permanently damaging it. The ship promptly went madly off in all directions. After a wild ride, it crashed into a nearby planet, forcibly ejected its occupants into the nearest solid land, and self-destructed in a fiery orange haze.

Jefferson and Hamilton looked with awe at the demise of their ship, and then again at the seemingly barren wasteland that lay before them, which they would now have to explore without a ship.

"Well, Ms. *Civilization*," said Jefferson, "now you're about to experience the *opposite* of that. This is the kind of universe I *thrive* in."

"What kind of place *is* this?" said the confused Hamilton.

"You should know, Star Soldier," Jefferson taunted, with her tongue sticking out.

"Don't start that again," Hamilton ordered. "Seriously: what are we getting into here? *You* should know *that*."

"Didn't you come around here before...?"

"No. I told you that already. I haven't."

"But surely you went down onto the planets that you were stationed at when you had the chance? Or didn't they let you do that?"

"Not as often as you think. When we were posted to places like this, it was always on the surface. We never went down unless we had to. And most of the time, we didn't."

"Like I said, I know these kind of places. You've been trying to civilize me, Hamilton. So let me try to wild you back."

Hamilton grimaced while she pocketed her gun, which she had held on to tightly and successfully during her recent scuffle.

"It's a good thing we're armed," said Hamilton. "You still got yours?"

"Yeah."

"Where'd you put it? I don't see it on you." Jefferson paused, cryptically.

"Well?" insisted Hamilton.

"I... don't think you want to know," responded Jefferson.

"Yeah," said Hamilton, ruefully. "I think I don't, after all. Let's just see if we can find Jackpot around here and get this collection thing done. Okay?"

Jefferson nodded in agreement, and they set off into the great unknown.

VI.

What followed was a small catalogue of action adventure science fiction clichés that don't need to be gone into in full at this moment. Suffice it to say, Jefferson had more than a few opportunities in the following hours to display the full extent of her enormous speed, intelligence and strength. When they were threatened by the various predatory cryptozoological oddities which inhabited the planet, Jefferson outfought and killed one and knocked several others out cold. On one of the rare occasion where this did not occur, Jefferson hoisted Hamilton onto her shoulders, and ran with such blinding speed that the beast pursuing them was in no way able to keep up with her. It might have been a clean getaway save for the fact that Jefferson ran through a heavily forested jungle, and Hamilton was knocked clean off of her back by a very large and stout tree limb. At which point, she was tightly constricted by a snake, which might have killed her- had Jefferson not constricted the snake with her paws instead.

Yet Hamilton, as well, had moments of glory. On another rare occasion when Jefferson's powers failed her, and she appeared on the point of being both eaten and consumed by her opponent, Hamilton saved the day by firing a point blank shot into the beast's chest. Likewise, on some of the occasions when Jefferson's courage seemed to fail her- though she insisted otherwise- Hamilton made it clear to her that they had come too far to abandon their prospects back home so easily, and they needed to continue onward. This was particularly effective when they were cornered at the edge of a very large waterfall, and had no other choice but to jump off of it, into the churning white foam at the bottom.

*

Remarkably, they survived this potentially fatal action. Jefferson overtook Hamilton during the fall, and was able to land at the base of a small cavern whose entrance was hidden by the falling water. Landing on her feet, she was able to catch Hamilton and place her safely on the ground beside her.

"Great," said Hamilton, sarcastically. "Another item off my bucket list. What now?"

"No point in looking back," said Jefferson. "We gotta go forward."

"Might as well," said Hamilton, sarcastically again. "What *else* could possibly go wrong?"

They stepped through the falling water and mist, to see what looked like an obscure trading post on the bend in the river nearest the falls. They went inside.

As they looked around, the alien behind the till, who resembled a bridle and saddle clad horse from the old days of Earth, made some disparaging remarks about the residents of that planet that she believed the pair would not overhear. She did not know of Jefferson Ball and her super canine abilities, or she would have been aware of the fact that her fur-covered ears could pick up things even normal canines, who already had very good hearing, could pick up on. Thus, upon hearing a particularly bad phrase emerge from the lips of the being, she went from her position on the shop floor to the till with quick speed even by her standards.

"*What* did you say?" Jefferson demanded.

"I didn't say *nothing*," retorted the being, in a hard-bitten, middle-aged female voice.

"Yes, you *did*," insisted Jefferson. "I *heard* you."

"With *that* hair? I shouldn't think you humans would hear anything under that."

"I'm a *dog*."

"Huh?"

"Don't you see the fur, the nose, the paws? And I have *ears* inside this rug, *thank you*, same as any other mammal. Ye gods! You thought I was *human*? How long has it been since you got any *civilized* people on this rock? We dogs took over from the humans a long time ago, to Earth's *benefit*, and you *bumpkins* better step up and recognize that!"

"Can I talk to you about this…outside?" said the alien.

"Why, sure," said Jefferson, surprisingly naïve all of a sudden, as they exited the shop and moved to the front lawn outside. "Why do we need to go….?"

Once they were outside, and the door shut, the alien proceeded to physically attack Jefferson, with a larger amount of force than Jefferson expected from such a small, compact body. Jefferson had no alternative but to defend herself, with both her own formidable strength and an equally formidable body of profane language. The alien proved to be more than a match for her in the latter category as much as she was in the former.

This was all unknown to Hamilton, and therefore unnoticed by her, other than the odd *thud* that happened when one of the outside gladiatorial combatants hit the side of one of the building's walls.

This was because she had found the proprietor of the place and was now seeking information from him. He was a small compact being, like his employee, consisting only, it appeared, of orange fur and big eyes. Adorning the body was a large green hat with a yellow sheriff's star prominently displayed on it, and somewhat garish colored shoes and socks on his feet.

"My associate and I," explained Hamilton, "are looking for a fellow named Jackpot Dingo, who owes an acquaintance of ours a large sum of money. We're supposed to either bring him, or the money, or both of them back to Earth. You know him?"

At the uttering of Jackpot's name, the proprietor shivered, something Hamilton could not fail to notice.

"Sho' have," he said, with an accent that suggested that he "really" came from somewhere in the southern United States, though he more likely picked up the English language through a traveling astronaut from that geographic area. "Only his tain't a good rep-pew-tation."

"That I know about. We've had past dealings with him."

"Not recent, like, though. Have ya?"

"Yeah. It's been a few years. Has he changed much from what he used to be like?"

"I wouldn't know much 'bout that. All I know is what I hear 'bout him now."

"And it's not the greatest, I suspect?"

"No. He seemed okay, at first, when he first come here. But, after a couple months..."

"What happened?"

"The *heat* done got him. You prob'ly noticed this place is hotter than most when ya landed here, didn't ya?"

"That," said Hamilton, ruefully, "was immediately apparent."

"Well, he gone stark raving bonkers. Plumb loco. Regular Tom O'Bedlam."

"Mad?"

"If ya wanna put it like that, then yeah."

"And not just that. He done made himself "king" of the nearby township, without consultin' not nobody what lives around here, and them. That ain't how it's done. We's supposed to be a dem-mo-cratic planet, here. But what's been gettin' me is the fact that he's been kittin' himself out with a reg'lar harereem!"

"That sounds like him. He tried to do the same thing when he was sane."

"But it's been mostly the gals of *mah* race. Don't know what they see in him, but it hurts *mah* matrimonial prospects considerable!"

"Well, if we can make things easier by getting rid of him, you'd be happy, then? Wouldn't you?" "Sho' would."

"Then tell me where he is right now, and we'll deal with him."

He did. After which a massive *thud* which neither of them could ignore hit the side of the building, rattling the very clapboard that served as its foundation. When the two of them got outside, they saw Jefferson, who had finally knocked out the alien horse, standing over her in triumph.

"And don't *ever* call me that *again*," she declared.

Looking at Hamilton and the proprietor, with the latter reflecting shock and the former face slapping embarrassment, Jefferson proceeded to clarify the source of the conflict.

"*She* started it."

Hamilton was too enraged to speak to Jefferson with mere words. Pulling out her gun, she pointed it at Jefferson, who was grinning in sheepish apology at the proprietor. After giving a sideways glance of embarrassed apology at the proprietor herself (and receiving a very sympathetic glance, in turn), Hamilton frog marched Jefferson off the property, while the proprietor tended to his fallen clerk.

VII.

Hamilton's wrath was short-lived. Once she felt Jefferson had been punished enough for her recent actions, she ordered her to stop and pocketed her gun again.

"We're about near where he said Jackpot's "kingdom" was, at any rate," Hamilton said, as she began to relax again. The thought of their "job" nearly being concluded pleased her.

"Him?" Jefferson sniggered. "A "king"? Please! Anybody 'round here can make themselves a "king" or

"queen" if they need an ego boost. Fairly easy in the less civilized parts of the universe."

"Really?" said Hamilton, who found that hard to swallow. "Are the beings out here really that gullible that they'll fall for a con man or woman's line of gab, and make them their monarch, just like that?"

"They were falling for it back when that human guy Kipling wrote about those two dumb Englishmen who got away with it out in Asia back in the 19th century," Jefferson answered. "Not much has really changed since then, based on my experience."

"Yeah. But that was a *story*. And they *didn't* get away with it, in the end."

"You read that one, too?"

"High school. Ancient human studies. It was my best subject."

"Mine, too. In the scholarly stuff, I mean. Small world. How come we never figured that we had that in common before?"

"Doesn't matter. We can talk more about it later. If we get out of here, that is. Right now, we got company to deal with. Look!"

Sure enough, a group of what could only be considered Jackpot's "wives" arrived on the scene. Like the proprietor of the store, they were beings that consisted of orange fur and big eyes, accompanied by grass skirts and bras made of what appeared to be halved coconuts. They spoke in the same manner as him, mumbling contemptuously under their breaths as they raised small but sharply pointed spears at them. Jefferson, at least, made a show of considering them intimidating "fiends" in her body movements, but Hamilton was less convinced.

"Are we supposed to fall for this cock and bull display?" she whispered to Jefferson.

"If we want to find Jackpot, then yeah," Jefferson whispered back. "This place is a bit behind the times, society wise."

"*That's* pretty obvious."

"Just let me deal with them. I know their language."

"I never figured you for a linguist," said Hamilton. "Well, not any sort of scholar at all, but..."

"Thank you for your confidence," said Jefferson, sarcastically. "Look. You know stuff and I know stuff. We don't necessarily know the *same* stuff, though. Let me deal with this 'cause it's in my line. Once we get into something that's in your bag, I'll tell you."

"Agreed."

Jefferson went to what appeared to be the head of the welcoming committee, and spoke to her.

"Y'all come with us, y'hear?" said the leader.

"Y'all addressing me and my friend, y'all?" retorted Jefferson.

"Yeah. Y'all state your bizness as we be goin'."

They started to walk towards what appeared to be the "kingdom".

"We," continued Jefferson, "be seekin' yer a-p'inted *leader*, y'all."

At the word "leader", the ladies- save for Jefferson and Hamilton- bowed down on the ground, in a feverish displayed of awed reverence.

"Why y'all be doin' that?" said Jefferson.

"Is y'all sick in the haid?" said the head alien. "We *gots* to."

"But I be askin' *why*, y'all? What power has he done got over the likes of y'all?"

"Y'all ain't never been 'round these parts before, has y'all?"

"Nope. Reckon this is my and my pal's first time in these parts."

"Then y'all ain't part of the clan of the all mighty Jackpot."

Hamilton threatened to laugh out loud, and extremely and derisively loudly, at that, after hearing the coupling of the adjective "all mighty" with the noun "Jackpot", but a glare from Jefferson stopped her just in time.

"No, we ain't," Jefferson continued. "He controls these parts, don't he?"

"I should say he does, y'all."

"And y'all are taking us to 'im, are y'all?"

"Yes, indeed. Y'all are our prisoners- and therefore his'n. He is the one true thing upon which the whole of this here powerful orb done revolve around, y'all."

"How'd he show y'all this was the gospel truth?"

"Why, he just came in out-a th' sky one day in his fire belching chariot, and got out of it with a powerful masculine stride that not nobody amongst us coulda matched. The *men* folks, ah mean. And he done displayed his great strength to us all by smashing a vessel of what was most undoubtedly am-brosy-a 'gainst the side of his head with like no trouble whatsoevah. And we knew right away that, from those very things, he done had to be *imm-MOR-tal*. He had 'zactly the lean and *hongry* look that proved it." "I don't follow," interjected Hamilton.

"He showed up in a spaceship one day, got out of it, drank a beer, and crumpled the aluminum can it was in against his head," translated Jefferson.

"And from *that* they decided to make him a king?"

"Others have become 'em over less."

"We'll let him 'splain it *to* you," interjected the boss lady. "Y'all better get goin' or we'll make y'all start *crawlin'* to him."

"Don't y'all worry about that," said Jefferson. To Hamilton, she added under her breath:

"...because *he's* the one who's gonna be crawling."

*

The "king" was in repose, lying sideways on his hastily constructed "throne", when Jefferson and Hamilton were ushered into see him. If Jefferson and Hamilton expected a more masculine and regal figure to be in charge of this jury rigged "kingdom", then they were soundly mistaken.

He immediately recognized Hamilton, at least. Jefferson, in her new and improved form, was a complete stranger to him. Therefore, as he saw it, she was a completely new opportunity for a "catch".

Jackpot as was a dog of the new modern Earth as Jefferson and Hamilton. But whereas Jefferson and

Hamilton could trace their ancestry back chiefly to both the wild and domesticated dogs of the North America of the old human Earth, Jackpot, as per his surname, was descended from the unique and wily wild canines who had once called the island cum continent of Australia home. He bore no trace of the particularly unmistakable Anglo-Irish accent the human residents of the continent once spoke with in his voice, this having expired along with that group of people. Rather, he spoke in the same fashion as Jefferson and Hamilton, in the uniform America centric dialect of English in which all of the canine peoples of Earth had to learn as their first language, for economic as well as sociopolitical reasons. But much of his thoughts and actions were driven by the survival standards his ancestors in the fabled "Outback" had once cultivated, just as Jefferson and Hamilton's ancestors had done similarly on the plains and in the mountains of North America. Which of theirs was the superior line of reasoning was yet to be proven.

Getting up, and giving a clap of his paws, which served as an order to his "wives" to temporarily disperse, he got up and walked towards them.

"Well," he said, addressing Hamilton. "This is a sight for sore eyes. Private Hamilton Pomeranian. How have you...?"

"*Major* Pomeranian," said that worthy. "We've been apart too long, Jackpot. I moved up in the ranks, like I said I would."

"My apologies," he said, bowing gentlemanly. "And who is...?" "Jefferson Ball," said that individual.

"I don't believe I know you," Jackpot said, seductively, to Jefferson, as she backed away from him temporarily. "I mean, once upon a time there was a girl I knew, rather briefly, who had that name. And then there's that adventuress with super powers who's been going around that..."

"I," said Jefferson, marching forward towards him, and barely restraining her anger, "am *both* of them!"

Suddenly, Jackpot realized exactly who and what he was dealing with. And that, his name to the contrary, his "luck" had run out. Especially when he turned from Jefferson towards Hamilton, who leveled her gun at him, and seemed intent on firing it.

"Thought you were so *smart*, huh?" said Hamilton. "Get off Earth, and all your problems were solved. That all space was your oyster, and you could twist it any way you wished. Maybe that was true back when we were all grunts, Jackpot. But not anymore. You owe a big amount of money back there, in case you *forgot* amongst your stately pleasure dome decreed here. And we've been sent to collect. If not you and the money, then just you. At least they have laws on Earth about where to put people who run out on their debts. The girls whose cherries you took should be so lucky."

"*That's* what this is about?" said Jackpot, indignantly. "I thought you'd be *grateful* to me that I went and did you that *favor* so long ago..."

Furiously, Jefferson grabbed him by the collars of the shirt and jacket he wore, and held on tight.

"That wasn't a *favor* to anybody but *you*," she snapped. "I could've gone without your "favor", you know. So could Ham. You didn't have to be our first. We each could have somebody *better-* who actually *cared* about us- do it when we *wanted* them to do it. The only reason you ended up being both of our first- and I don't know how many others, besides- was because you *tricked* us. Same as you tricked all the men out of their freshly earned pocket change. Same as you tricked D.T. out of that money- none of which you still *have* on you, of course?" He nodded negatively.

"I didn't think so. What have you got to say about that?" She dropped him on the ground.

"I was *gonna* pay D.T. back," he said. "Only the girls found me when I landed, and thought I was some sort of God or something, and then they...."

"What in the hell were you going to pay him back *with*?" demanded Hamilton. "Jefferson and I have been traveling for *days* here, and there's nothing resembling a BANK in sight!"

"Ah, but that's where the natural resources of this place come in," Jackpot said, in a reverie that suggested that his sanity was either lost or gone. "They'll pay off all my debts, easily."

"Natural resources?" Jefferson sounded contemptuously skeptical. "Do you see any "natural resources" here, Ham?"

"Not unless you count the enormous capacity for hydroelectricity that waterfall we fell over might have," mused Hamilton. "Provided, of course, it was handled the right way. But I doubt that's what you meant, is it, Jackpot?"

"No. You don't get it. Let me show you."

He spent the next few minutes showing them storehouses of potential wealth encased in the very land and water of the planet. A stream which ran liquid mercury instead of water, and was studded with innumerable diamonds, rubies, and emeralds of prodigious size. A cavern, in which massive crystallized stalagmites hung from the roof, and were capable of falling and granting the dreams of wealth of anyone who was able to claim them at any minute. To say nothing of the wide hills overtop the cavern, in which you could not even walk without stumbling over a golden nugget or a silver deposit the likes of which had not been seen on Earth in at least a millennia.

All of which were simply inventions of his mind, which had once been rational enough to charm anyone in his sights into believing anything he said to them, but was now completely and utterly insane.

Finally, Jefferson cut him off when he tried to convince of the existence of another "wonder" of the planet as they returned from viewing the others.

"I don't think we ought to waste any more of your time, and *ours,*" she concluded, trying to humor him. "It's all pretty interesting, but you forgot one thing." "What's that?" he said.

"The exchange rate. The farther away from Earth something comes in, the higher it'll be taxed."

"You can't mean that," he said, his hopes finally dashed. "When'd they bring that in?"

"After you left," said Hamilton. "They also made it illegal to run out on your debts. Which is what you're facing when we take you back, and what you deserve. And don't think it'll help you if you plead the fact that you ran up the debts *before* the law came in. They don't buy that. You're facing serious time, Jackpot, and you can't con your way out of it. We're taking you back with us-so you can finally face what you deserve for everything you did to me and Jefferson and everyone else!"

"Not if I *kill* you first!"

Before either of them could react, Jackpot knocked the gun out of Hamilton's paws, and began advancing towards her. With intent to kill, or worse.

As Hamilton was less than half his size, and she was too shocked and scared by his actions to fully defend herself, it looked like she was finished if he caught and grabbed her, which could be as soon as their next heartbeats. She backed up as far and as fast she could, but it wasn't enough. He moved faster than her, and seemed intent on catching her.

He'd reckoned without Jefferson, however. She threw her powerful paws around his neck and squeezed with all the strength she had. It took only a moment for his half naked body to hit the ground, dead.

Recovering her wits- and her gun- Hamilton surveyed her friend's actions.

"Wow," she said. "You killed him. Single pawed."

"He started it," was all Jefferson would say in response.

*

In another remarkable occurrence, they managed to find Jackpot's spaceship, which the aliens, in shock over the besting over their "leader", let them have as the "conquerors" of said person. It was, fortunately, one of the kind of spaceship that was, while beaten up a little, still serviceable and usable.

They cleaned it up a little and then flew off, with Hamilton at the controls.

"I really owe you now, Jeff," she said.

"How so?" Jefferson replied.

"D-uh. The *obvious* thing. You saved me from being *murdered* by a deranged lunatic."

"Who laid and left us both, back when he had what passed for a mind. You are very welcome. It's not the first time I've done it, but it is the first time in saving *your* life since we reconnected. But what I don't understand is why you didn't shoot him when you had the chance."

"I didn't think he was gonna try to kill me. He always said he was a lover and not a fighter."

"Even a lover can turn fighter when it matters. Me, for example."

"Yeah. But I wasn't ready. And I don't think I've ever been that vulnerable before. I always had the gun and the Star Soldier uniform before to protect me. And then I had just the one thing, and then I was without even that...Why, he could have...I can't even begin to think about what he might have..."

"You still had your mind. Which was more than he had left."

"Never mind him, now. He's gone. What are we gonna tell D.T.?"

"About him not getting the money back? We tell him the truth. That Jackpot went nuts. That he got stuck on that planet, and that he thought there was fabulous wealth there. And he went and drank his own Kool Aid about that, since he was so used to have other people believe it when it gave it to *them*."

"Are you sure D.T.'d be okay with it? It seemed like he'd be willing to rip us apart if we didn't bring

Jackpot *and* all of the money back."

"You don't know him like I do."

"Right. I don't."

"That whole threaten to kill you *schtick* is just for show, just to show you he means business. If you're honest with him and don't coat it with B.S., he'll get it."

"And he'll pay us like he said?"

"Why, certainly. Unlike the late Mr. Jackpot, he doesn't welch out on deals."

"Just like we don't either. Do we, *partner*?"

"Of course we don't, *partner.*"

And, with dreams of a rosy financial future, at least for the time being, they flew back, as soon as it was possible, to Earth.

About the Author

David Perlmutter is a freelance writer based in Winnipeg, Manitoba, Canada. He is the author of two books on animation history: America 'Toons In: A History of Television Animation (McFarland and Co.) and The Encyclopedia Of American Animated Television Shows (Rowman and Littlefield), as well as essays and works of speculative fiction. .